Gingerbread Man

by Fran Hunia

illustrated by Brian Price Thomas

Ladybird Books

A little old man

and a little old woman

have a house on a farm.

All children have
a great ambition to read
to themselves...

and a sense of achievement when they can do so.
The **read it yourself** *series has been devised to*
satisfy their ambition. Since many children learn
from the Ladybird Key Words Reading Scheme,
these stories have been based to a large extent
on the Key Words List, and the tales chosen are
those with which children are likely to be familiar.

The series can of course be used as supplementar
reading for any reading scheme.

Gingerbread Man is intended for children reading
to Book 4c of the Ladybird Reading Scheme. The
following words are additional to the vocabulary
used at that level —

gingerbread, fox, old, woman, over
soon, cooked, out, of, can't, runs,
eat, swim, tail, feet, back, again,
head, nose, SNAP, gulp, went

Published by Ladybird Books Ltd Loughborough Leicestershire UK
Ladybird Books Inc Auburn Maine 04210 USA

Printed in England

Two children come to help

on the farm.

The little old woman says

to the children,

"I want to make you

some good things for tea.

Do you want a big cake

or a gingerbread man?"

"We like gingerbread,"

say the children.

"Please make us

a gingerbread man."

The little old woman
makes a gingerbread man.

She puts him in the oven
and then she gets on
with her work.

9

Soon the gingerbread man
is cooked. The little old woman
gets him out of the oven.

"What a good gingerbread man,"
she says. "The children can have him
for tea."

The gingerbread man looks up.

"No, no, they can't," he says.

"No one will have me for tea."

He jumps down and runs off.

"Stop, stop,"

says the little old woman.

"No, I will not stop,

and you can't get me,"

says the gingerbread man,

and he runs out of the house.

The little old man is at work
on the farm.

He sees the gingerbread man.
"Stop, little gingerbread man,"
he says.
"The children want to have you
for tea."

"No, no," says the gingerbread man

"I will not stop for you.

The little old woman can't get me,

and you can't get me.

No one will have me for tea."

The gingerbread man runs on.

16

The children see

the gingerbread man.

"Stop, little gingerbread man,"

they say. "We want to have you

for tea."

"No, no," says the gingerbread man

"I will not stop for you.

The little old woman can't get me,

the little old man can't get me,

and you can't get me.

No one will have me for tea."

He runs on.

A horse sees the gingerbread man.

"Stop, little gingerbread man,"

he says. "Let me have you

for my tea."

"No, no," says the gingerbread man.

"I will not stop for you.

The little old woman can't get me,

the little old man can't get me,

the children can't get me,

and you can't get me.

No one will have me for tea."

He runs on.

A cow sees the gingerbread man.

"Stop, little gingerbread man,"

she says. "I want

to have you for my tea."

"No, no," says the gingerbread man

"I will not stop for you.

The little old woman can't get me,

the little old man can't get me,

the children can't get me,

the horse can't get me,

and you can't get me.

No one will have me for tea."

He runs on.

A dog sees the gingerbread man.

" Stop, little gingerbread man,"

he says. " Let me eat you up

for tea."

"No, no," says the gingerbread man

"I will not stop for you.

The little old woman can't get me,

the little old man can't get me,

the children can't get me,

the horse can't get me,

the cow can't get me,

and you can't get me.

No one will have me for tea."

He runs on.

A cat sees the gingerbread man.

"Stop, little gingerbread man,"

says the cat. "I want

to eat you up."

"No, no," says the gingerbread man.

"I will not stop for you.

The little old woman can't get me,

the little old man can't get me,

the children can't get me,

the horse can't get me,

the cow can't get me,

the dog can't get me,

and you can't get me.

No one will have me for tea."

He runs on.

The gingerbread man comes

to some water.

"What can I do?" he says.

"There is no boat here,

and I can't swim.

The cat and the dog and the cow

and the horse and the children

and the little old man

and the little old woman

all want to eat me,

and I can't get away."

A fox comes up.

"Let me help you," he says.

"I can swim into the water

with you on my tail.

There will be no danger.

Come on. Jump on my tail."

The gingerbread man thanks the fox and jumps up on his tail.

Away they go into the water.

The gingerbread man can not

keep his feet out of the water.

"Please help me. My feet

are in the water," he says.

"Then get on my back,"

says the fox.

The gingerbread man

jumps on the fox's back,

and the fox swims on.

Soon the gingerbread man's feet
are in the water again.

"Please help me. My feet
are in the water," he says.

"Then get up on my head,"
says the fox.

The gingerbread man thanks
the fox and jumps up on his head.

The fox swims on.

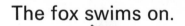

Soon the gingerbread man's feet
are in the water again.

"Please help me. My feet
are in the water," he says.

"Then get up on my nose,"
says the fox.

The gingerbread man jumps up
on the fox's nose.

Then SNAP!
The fox eats him up
in one big gulp.

Then there was no gingerbread

man for the cat or the dog

or the cow or the horse

or the children or the little old man

or the little old woman,

and they all went home again.